minedition

English edition published 2012 by Michael Neugebauer Publishing Ltd., Hong Kong
distributed in GB by BOUNCE! Sales and Marketing Ltd., London

Text and Illustrations copyright © 2012 Judith Loske
Original Title: Der Koffer, die Katze und die Tuba
Coproduction with Michael Neugebauer Publishing Ltd., Hong Kong.

Manufactured in China.
Typesetting in Eras
Colour separation by HiFai, Hong Kong
A CIP Catalogue record for this book is available from the British Library

ISBN 978-988-15953-4-8
10 9 8 7 6 5 4 3 2 1
First Impression

For more information please visit our website: www.minedition.com

Judith Loske
A Suitcase, a Cat, and a Tuba

minedition

Lottie had a suitcase.
It was a big, old, brown leather suitcase and it was a
gift from Grandpa. It was so big that it almost reached
her belly button - and it was full of secret finds.

These secret finds were the things that Lottie had discovered.
Sometimes she found them on the street, or in the grass,
or even on the bus.
She would put each new treasure in her suitcase.

Lottie wore the key to the suitcase around her neck.
This way her secrets would stay secret.
But sometimes Lottie wished there was someone
with whom she could share her secrets.

The other children found Lottie odd
and her suitcase... ugly.

She often annoyed the neighbouring children.
When they ran after her shouting nasty words, she would
run into the back garden of her house hugging her
suitcase tightly.

One day Lottie saw Leon, the boy next door,
sitting alone.
Every day Leon played his tuba, secretly, between
the clothes drying on the line.
Lottie liked his music.
But today there was no music; today it was quiet.
"Mozart has disappeared," said Leon.
"I've looked everywhere."

Mozart was Leon's fat cat. Lottie had often seen Leon talking to his cat.

And the cat meowing back to Leon. Perhaps they told each other secrets?

Leon told her how much Mozart liked to sleep curled up beside him in bed.
The cat was always telling him stories. Leon didn't understand them, but the sound made him happy.
The cat often sat with him when Leon played his tuba.
Mozart watched Leon's fingers as they hopped over the keys.

Lottie felt as if she had known Leon
forever.
She moved a little closer to him.
Her heart was pounding.

She took her key and opened the suitcase.
"These things tell stories just like Mozart,"
whispered Lottie.
"You just have to listen closely."
Leon listened.

"Do you know the feeling of walking through the wet grass and suddenly finding the abandoned home of a snail?" said Lottie.

"Stones are all different. Most are not even similar.
I wonder where this stone has been and who has
held it in their hand?"

"Maybe a flying bird lost this feather and it floated
down to earth, gently turning and spinning all
the way?"

"If you hold a shell to your ear," whispered Leon, "you can hear the sound of the waves, magically, right here, in the middle of the city!"

Lottie smiled.

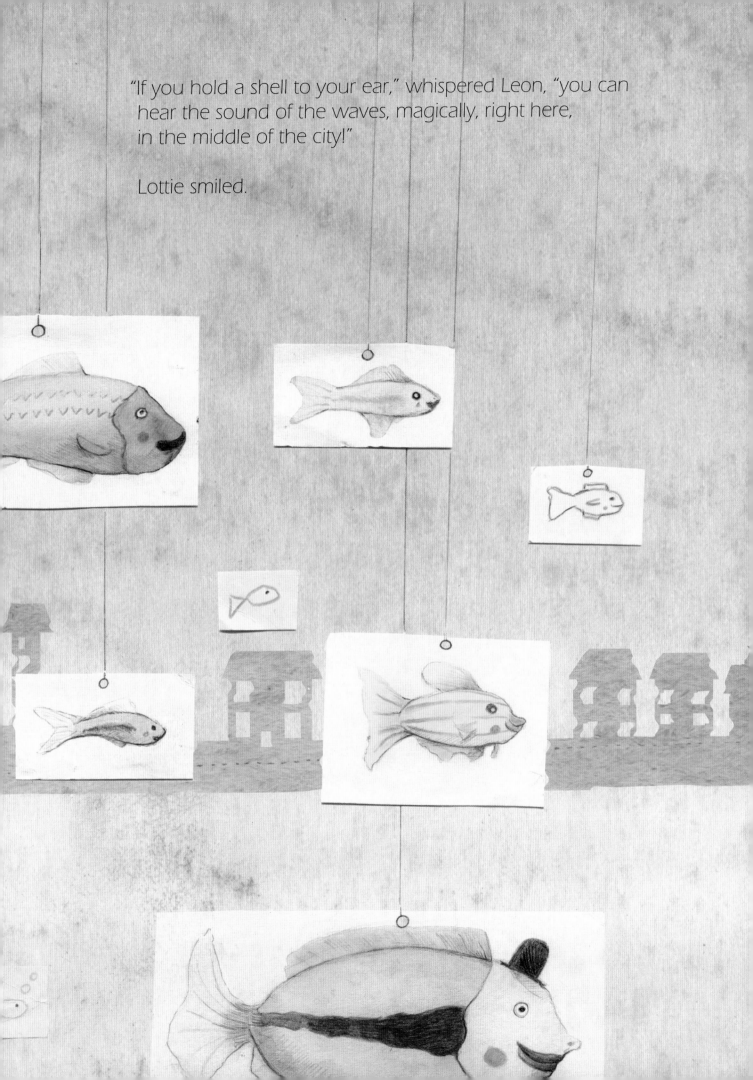

Leon picked up his tuba and began to play.
Lottie was enchanted by his music
and she was not the only one!
As if by magic it brought the sounds of the sea
        right into the middle of the city.